UNDERWORLDS

REVENGE OF THE
SCORPION KING

TO DYLAN
CRANSTON,
MAY THE MYTHS
BE WITH YOU

ISBN 978-0-545-30833-5

Text copyright © 2012 by Robert T. Abbott

Illustrations copyright © 2012 by Scholastic Inc.

All rights reserved. Published by Scholastic Inc.

SCHOLASTIC and associated logos are trademarks
and/or registered trademarks of Scholastic Inc.

12 11 10 9 8 7 6 5 4 3 2 1   12 13 14 15 16 17/0

Printed in the U.S.A.   40
First printing, August 2012
DESIGNED BY TIM HALL

UNDERWORLDS

BOOK THREE

REVENGE OF THE SCORPION KING

BY **TONY ABBOTT**

ILLUSTRATED BY

ANTONIO JAVIER CAPARO

Scholastic Inc.

RIVER STYX

ARENA

GREEK

HADES'
THRONE

NORSE

EGYPTIAN

BABYLONIAN

TOWER

EUPHRATES
RIVER

WALL

TIGRIS
RIVER

CHAPTER ONE

—

MYTHS R US

JON DOYLE POKED ME IN THE RIBS. "OWEN, WE SHOULD really hide."

"We *are* hiding," I said, "behind this very big sand dune."

"I mean hide *better*," he said. "So we don't die."

Jon had a way with words.

Sydney Lamberti peeked over the sand dune and slid back down. "Jon's right," she said. "Those guys aren't just regular Underworld soldiers. They have nasty lion heads. And long swords. And they brought a big ugly *thing* with them."

Underworld soldiers. Lion heads. A big ugly *thing*.

This was my life right now.

Ignoring the fact that my brain was spinning nonstop, I peered over the crest of the dune and tried to focus.

It was nighttime, and the crescent moon shone in the black sky like a jewel. But even in the pale darkness, the big ugly *thing* was easy to spot because it took up so much space.

"He looks like a serpent," I said. "A cross between a dragon and a giant crocodile."

Dana Runson edged up beside me. "He's coming really fast —"

WHOOM!

The air roared like a thousand jet engines, and green flames shot out of the serpent's mouth like a cannonball. Just like that, our hiding place wasn't there anymore.

"Get — out — of — here!" cried Jon.

We turned and ran across the sand. That's fairly hard for people to do, but apparently it's what Babylonian Underworld monsters are built for. The serpent's four webbed feet clawed the ground like propellers as he leaped over the dunes.

WHOOM! The sand to our left crackled and went shiny in the moonlight.

"Glass!" Sydney said. "He just turned the sand into glass! I don't want to be glass! Run this way —"

The sand exploded in front of her.

"Run the other way!"

We jumped over the top of the next dune and rolled down the other side. Then we zigzagged right and left until we heard the serpent's thundering steps slow to a stop.

We huddled at the base of a big dune and all held our breath. A slow minute went by.

"No sound," Dana whispered. "I can't look. Did we lose him?"

My stomach flip-flopped as we crawled up to peek over the sand. Not twenty yards away the serpent stood on his hind legs, moving his head back and forth. It was clear that he couldn't see very well, but his snout was snorting in and out as if it were a bellows.

"He's trying to smell us," I whispered.

"Humans sweat, and sweat smells," said Sydney, sliding down the dune. "The glands in our skin give off sweat when we're running for our lives."

"Thank you, Encyclopedia Syd," said Jon.

Sydney thinks and talks a little like a computer sometimes, even when there are more important things to worry about.

Beyond the serpent marched a long column of warriors. They were bigger than regular men — just our luck! — and each of their heads had the snout and long, shaggy mane of a jungle lion. Great.

"Halt!" one of the guards growled, and the soldiers surrounded a wooden sledge with long, curved rails that looked a little like a Santa's sleigh. Except I knew that its owner, Loki, was the exact opposite of friendly old Santa. Loki was an evil Norse trickster, determined to overthrow Odin, the Norse god who lived in the mythological world of Asgard.

Myths were my life now, too.

"The soldiers are bringing the sledge into the city," Dana whispered.

The city.

A few minutes earlier, we'd watched as Loki and his wolf, Fenrir, had entered the gates of that city. We'd soon realized that it was the capital of the Babylonian Underworld. Surrounded by a massive wall of amber stone and marked with a series of tall blue gates, the city must have been hundreds of square miles in size. It looked like the world's largest, oldest, most terrifying prison. A single tower stood just inside the walls and rose up into the black sky, as if it might touch the moon.

Sydney tapped my shoulder. "The serpent is still sniffing. I say we don't move."

"Good plan," I said.

I didn't want to move.

I didn't want to do anything.

Only a few hours before, Sydney, Dana, Jon, and I had been more or less safe in our little town of Pinewood Bluffs.

I say "more or less," because we'd been in the pro-
cess of returning a pair of escaped Cyclopes — the
one-eyed giants of Greek mythology — to Hades'
Underworld, whose entrance was under our school.
No big deal, right? Once we did that, we were about
to go home and call it a day when we spotted Loki
slipping away in his sledge.

We already knew that Loki was cruel, sly, and dangerous. But after the Cyclopes made him a suit of
magical armor, he became practically indestructible.

Loki was now the complete evil package.

Probably because we were too tired to think straight
after wrangling the giants, we decided we couldn't just
let Loki escape. So we stowed away on his sledge.

Brilliant, huh?

Not so much. Because before we knew it, we were
in the crazy, evil Babylonian Underworld hiding from
a big ugly *thing*.

"Loki must be after the seven fire monsters of
Babylonian mythology," Dana said, gazing at the city
and tapping a finger on her beat-up copy of *Bulfinch's
Mythology*. "Remember what we heard him say?"

How could we forget?

The horned, the clawed, the fanged.

All of them will join me.

"*Bulfinch's* doesn't have any Babylonian stories in it," Dana said, scanning the margins of the book's tattered pages, "but luckily, I took lots of notes from my parents' library."

Dana's parents were in Iceland, on the hunt for something called the Crystal Rune, which Loki needed in his war against Odin.

"I'm pretty sure that creature is called Fire Serpent," Dana said, rifling through the pages of her book. "In fact, most of the Babylonian monsters have something to do with fire."

Clank! The lion-headed warriors hitched a pair of heavy chains to Loki's sledge. With a growl from their commander, they dragged the sledge across the sand toward the nearest blue gate.

The serpent didn't go with them.

Jon slumped down the dune and sighed a long, slow breath. "I don't want to say it, but I think we need to get past the serpent and inside that scary city. We have to stop Loki from collecting more monsters, even if it, you know, kills us, or something."

That was a lot of words for Jon. I guess he was nervous. Actually, *nervous* didn't cover. it. Terrified was more like it. Also crazy. Confused. Exhausted.

So were the rest of us.

"Jon, we'll be all right," I said.

"We'd better be," he said. "I have stuff to do before class on Monday." He took a deep breath and turned to Dana. "So where is Fire Serpent on the Babylonian scale of creepy?"

She scanned her scribbled notes. "There's one called Thornviper. And another known as Mad Dog. There's also something called Furnace."

Sydney sighed. "Nice."

At least we had some help.

We had an old lyre made by the ancient Greek musician Orpheus. I could play it a little, and its notes seemed to do magical things. Maybe more important, Dana had stolen one of Loki's armored gloves — which was both good and bad. The good part was that she could shoot bolts of lightning from its fingers.

The bad part was that it had grown over her hand and wouldn't come off. Oh, and Loki could sense when the glove was near, which almost gave us away on the sledge. Luckily, I was able to figure out the right notes to play on the lyre, which somehow shielded us.

Together, my lyre and Dana's glove had helped us escape a miserable death a few times already. I really hoped they would keep doing that.

"Fire Serpent on the move," Sydney whispered.

We slid to the bottom of the dune and backed away slowly until we heard the quiet lapping of water.

"If this Underworld is set up like the ancient empire of Babylon," said Dana, "then this could be the Tigris River —"

WHOOM!

Hot green flames suddenly blasted the sand behind us. Fire Serpent leaped over the top of the dune.

"Into the river!" Jon shouted.

We tumbled, rolled, ran, and fell down the dunes all the way to the riverbank. But the serpent had our scent and was hot on our heels. Really hot.

WHOOM! The riverbed exploded, showering us with wet sand. *WHOOM!* The reeds on the bank burst into flame.

Clutching the lyre's holster to my chest, I dived into the river just as — *WHOOM!* — a fist of green flame roared over our heads.

I swam underwater and kept myself submerged until I felt the water cool off downstream. I was about to pop up for air when I felt a sudden force on my back, keeping me down. I kicked and thrashed, trying to free myself, but the pressure was too strong.

I glimpsed Dana, Sydney, and Jon swimming toward me, but whatever was on my back forced me deeper under the surface. My lungs burned. My chest felt like bursting. Finally, I couldn't hold my breath anymore.

My lips opened in a rush of bubbles, and the space in front of my eyes went black.

CHAPTER TWO

BREATHLESS

AN INSTANT LATER, I SHOT UP OUT OF THE WATER, gasping for air. There was a splash next to me.

"I'll get the others," a voice growled.

"What — who —" I sputtered.

"Shhh! The serpent will hear you!"

Before I could see who was talking, there was another splash and I was alone.

I sucked in mouthfuls of air over and over. I shook my head and blinked my eyes. I saw . . . what *did* I see?

I was surrounded by a cluster of tall reeds somewhere downriver from the serpent.

Splash! Jon, Dana, and Sydney exploded up next to me, gasping and gurgling.

Jon coughed. "What is going on —"

"Shhh!" the voice growled again. "The serpent will give up if he doesn't hear us."

Standing there was a creature with the head of a lion. Water was dripping from his mane as he held up a paw.

Dana raised her silver glove warily. "Who exactly are you?"

"Just the guy who saved your lives," the lion-headed creature whispered. "Hush."

The roars of the serpent gradually faded. A long minute later, we heard the distant *boom* of the gate. The lion-headed creature relaxed. "They're back in the city. We're safe."

His voice wasn't as deep as the warriors we'd seen before, and his mane was short, not fully grown. I guessed maybe he was a boy.

"You know, you're pretty lucky you ran into me," he said. "Most strangers aren't dealt with kindly. And by that, I mean kkkkk!" He ran his finger under his furry chin. "Allow me to introduce myself. I am Panu, chief guard of the Eighth Gate of the Babylonian Underworld."

We stared at him for what seemed like an hour before Sydney finally spoke. "Okay. Panu. Well, thanks. For saving us, I mean."

"Wait. According to legend, aren't there only seven gates in the Babylonian Underworld?" asked Dana, tapping her book.

Her notes were *good*.

The lion-boy snorted. "It's an unofficial position. But I *will* be a guard one day. And as a future guard of our city, may I ask what you are doing here?"

We went quiet again.

"How do we know you won't turn us in?" I asked. "I mean, we know it's pretty much a crime to mess around in an Underworld when we . . . haven't been invited."

Panu wrinkled his snout into what I guessed was a smile. "Only when you want to leave. There are rules against leaving."

I didn't like how that sounded, either, but once again it was Sydney who broke the ice. "We're here because of Loki," she said.

Panu narrowed his large lion eyes. "The silver man? I saw him enter the city."

"He's evil," I said.

"There's plenty of evil here, believe me," said Panu.

"Loki is a Norse god," Dana put in. "And he's here to recruit the Babylonian monsters for his war against a bigger god. He plans to use our world as a stepping-stone."

"He'll destroy it to smithereens," said Jon.

Panu frowned. "I knew I didn't like the look of him. He'll want the fire monsters. They're famous in the Underworlds. You've already met Fire Serpent."

"Who nearly charbroiled us," said Syd. "Good thing he can't see."

"Stone blind," said Panu. "But his nose is as sensitive as it is ugly. He lives in the tower with the others." He paused for a minute. "If you want Loki, I can get you into the city. Come with me." He waded through the reeds and up the riverbank toward the dunes.

"This seems almost too easy," I said.

"We have to trust him, a little," whispered Sydney.

"I think he's cool," said Jon. "That hair is awesome."

Dana and I exchanged looks.

"Let's go with him, but be on our guard," she said, nodding.

With that, we followed Panu up the bank and across the dunes.

The tower that rose up from the city seemed more and more enormous as we got closer. Bonfires inside the walls cast wobbly golden light up the sides of the tower, and for the first time we saw gardens of vines and flowers hanging from the top all the way to the ground. Then it struck me.

"Guys, we're looking at the Hanging Gardens of Babylon!" I said. "One of the Seven Wonders of the Ancient World!"

Jon stared at the tower. "If only this were on a test. It's the one answer I'd get right."

Panu beamed as we wove between the dunes. "The hanging gardens are famous. The seven gates to the Underworld are also pretty well-known. Plus there are seven monsters, one for each of the seven levels of the Great Tower."

"Seven must be a special number in mythology," Jon said. "Owen's lyre has seven strings, too."

I carefully removed the lyre from its holster and checked it over. It was dry, and the strings were as tight as when I'd first held it.

Panu looked at the lyre closely. "Have you ever heard of the lost chord? It's a Babylonian legend about a bunch of notes that contain really powerful magic."

"Not really," I said. "I'm just learning how to use this."

Panu nodded. "The chord is lost, but the legend says that 'Only what is lost can be found.' Strange, right?"

I didn't know anything about the lost chord. All I knew was that Orpheus's lyre was magical . . . and incredibly handy. If you played it properly, you could make people and things do whatever you wanted. But its magic had a dark side, too. Whenever I plucked the strings, I got wobbly and my head felt like it was going to blow up. Not the best side effect.

"This way," said Panu, leading us quickly along the outside of the wall, past two of the gates. "Stay close. The guards have night vision. They have to, since it's always night here."

Jon frowned and mumbled, "Eagle-eyed lion-heads."

ROOOOO!

A loud bellow echoed inside the city. Panu paused and looked up at the tower.

"Is that one of the monsters?" Sydney asked.

Panu shook his head. "No, that's Kingu. He was a famous warrior who used to command the fire monsters. But he led them against Marduk, the great god of the Babylonian empire. So Marduk cursed him and his monsters to the Underworld and turned him into . . . something else." He was quiet for a moment. "He is cursed to remain in the Underworld, a prisoner of the monsters he used to rule."

Looking into the eyes of a lion was a strange feeling, but I saw how expressive they could be. Panu felt sorry for this Kingu guy, even though he had battled the gods.

"Loki wants those monsters," said Sydney, getting back to business. "He'll use his runes to get to them."

"Runes?" said Panu.

"Stones with magic symbols carved on them," Dana explained. "They're very old and powerful."

Panu frowned. "I don't like the sound of runes. But you have magic, too. The lyre. And this?" He pointed to the silver glove on Dana's hand.

"A little," Dana said, shrugging. She held her gloved hand close to her side, trying not to show how much it hurt. But I knew that the glove caused her as much pain as the lyre did me. The glove was super-useful, but part of me couldn't wait until she was free of it.

"Here we are." Panu paused at a section of the wall marked with decorative stones. He twisted one, pushed another, tapped a third, and a block in the wall moved aside smoothly to reveal a passage.

"Not bad, huh?" Panu ducked into the passage, and we followed him inside the city. The air instantly became stifling and hot and close, as if we had entered a sealed oven.

Zigging and zagging through the city streets to avoid patrols of armed guards, we soon found ourselves in a wide, moonlit courtyard. Flaming torches shone

BABYLONIAN UNDERWORLD

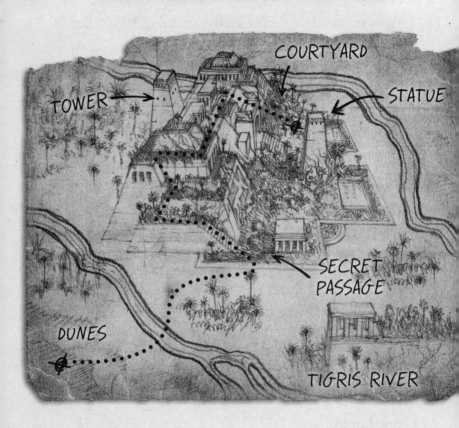

COURTYARD

TOWER

STATUE

SECRET PASSAGE

DUNES

TIGRIS RIVER

on the statue of a horrible beast with a winged head and a long beak.

"That's Marduk, the god who cursed Kingu," Panu said with a scowl. "A constant reminder of the failed war. Kingu says he's going to get his revenge the moment he's free."

Everything in this place was beautiful — the sand, the stone, the tower. But I was getting the feeling that the night wasn't the only dark thing here. There was a lot of anger and cruelty. Curses and revenge. And now Loki was in the mix.

The perfect ingredients for one colossal mess.

Careful to keep hidden from the guards on the city wall, we crept around the edge of the courtyard. The hot night was heavy with the sickly sweet smell of the vines and blossoms hanging from the tower.

Until the smell was covered by something else.

"Ugh, what is that stink?" whispered Panu, waving the air in front of his nose.

Sydney shuddered. "It's Fenrir!"

"Loki's wolf!" Jon gasped. "Hide!"

CHAPTER THREE

ETERNAL NIGHT

"INSIDE THE STATUE!" PANU DIRECTED US.

"Inside — ?" Dana said.

"It's hollow!" Panu swung open a compartment on the back of the statue, tugged us inside, and pulled the door closed.

Through the flaring nostrils of the statue's beak we saw Fenrir pad warily into the courtyard.

Fenrir was three times the size of any normal wolf and had wiry red fur, a head as big as a garbage can, and breath that smelled like one. Each fang was at least a foot long, his yellow eyes burned with a sickly fever, and he breathed stinky flames. He was not your standard wolf.

Just behind Fenrir strode Loki himself, and I felt my heart sink. Looking as if he owned the place, his expression cold and cruel, Loki seemed more evil than ever. The torchlight reflected off his powerful armor, which shone as brightly as the moon overhead.

I thumbed the lyre's lowest string gently, to mask the presence of Dana's stolen glove. It barely made a sound, but I knew it worked when Loki ignored the statue and turned to the shadows behind him.

"My dear Kingu, lord of the legendary fire monsters," he said icily, "join me on my journey to Asgard, the throne of the Norse gods. The trek will begin soon, and you will prove very useful."

The sound of Loki's voice made my skin crawl, and I felt Dana tense beside me. We all knew that Loki's "journey to Asgard" was code for his war against Odin.

A low voice emerged from the shadows across the

courtyard. "I tell you again, Loki, my curse prevents me from leaving the Underworld. I am a prisoner."

A figure moved in the shadows, and a sharp scent stung through the openings of the statue.

"That's the smell of venom," whispered Panu. "Now prepare yourselves. . . ."

Kingu, ruler of the fire monsters, entered the courtyard. The torch flames instantly dimmed. But even in the darkness, there was no mistaking what he was.

A giant insect.

Kingu's body, over ten feet tall, was formed of overlapping black plates that shifted as he moved. His legs — eight of them — looked like jackhammers, hinged with massive talons on the ends. He had industrial-size pincers for arms. His head was enormous, knobby, and angled, and his jaws looked like mechanical claws. Each large eye was yellow and deep, like fire blazing at the end of a long tunnel.

Jon gasped. "He's a . . . bug!"

"Scorpion," whispered Panu. "The Great God cursed him into the shape of a deadly desert scorpion. Kingu

SCORPION KING

is now the Scorpion King. He lives as a prisoner in the Underworld."

It was the long, thick tail arching up behind him that freaked me out the most. It split into two points, with a claw-tipped, venom-filled stinger on the end of each one. The stingers twitched and moved back and forth, as if they could see everything going on. Creepy.

"Time is of the essence," Loki said.

"Is it?" Kingu clacked his pincers, and two lion-headed soldiers walked in, carrying an ornate box between them. "The moon rises, falls, rises, falls. It is eternal night in my Underworld. I am cursed to remain here, staring at the heavens and seeing only darkness."

"I seek my revenge on Odin," said Loki. "He wounded me once, long ago. It was the last time he will do so. Your beasts — and you — can aid me."

Kingu nodded at the soldiers. They opened the box, then withdrew. "I also seek revenge against a great god. When I am free, all gods shall bow in fear."

With a strange pinging sound, a motorized bird rose from the box. It flapped its metal wings and circled the courtyard swiftly.

Zap!

One of Kingu's tail stingers shuddered, and the motorized bird fell to the ground like a stone. Loki's eyes darkened when a second bird flew up out of the box. "Help me now, Kingu, and I will help you. . . ."

Zap! The second bird fell.

Loki's expression was frozen as he watched a third bird take flight. I tried to see Kingu's stingers moving, but they were too fast.

"You may not have heard of the Twilight of the Gods, Kingu," Loki said. "It is the final battle and the defeat of Odin. It has been predicted."

"Warring against gods is dangerous," Kingu said. "I am proof of that, cursed to an eternity of darkness."

Zap! The third bird fell.

"Yes," said Loki, clenching and unclenching his one gloved fist. "But soon I will have a weapon to conquer all weapons."

Dana caught her breath. "The Crystal Rune," she whispered. "He'd better not hurt my parents. . . ."

"The final battle begins with the fabled Fires of Midgard," Loki went on, petting Fenrir's wiry fur.

"Midgard," said Kingu. "Is that not your name for the middle world, the world of humans?"

They were talking about our world. My blood went to ice all over again.

"In order for me to reach Odin's great hall, all of Midgard must burn to ash," said Loki frostily.

"Burn!" Sydney whispered in my ear. "That's why he wants the fire monsters. It all makes sense. . . ."

"The fire monsters of Babylon's Underworld are renowned among all beasts," Loki continued, looking sharply at Kingu. "Immortal. Angry. Destructive. I need all of them. And you, of course."

Kingu eyed a fourth bird as it circled the court-yard and settled on the end of the statue's beak. Jon pulled back.

"I understand," Kingu said. "But I am bound to the Great Tower. At the top are the Tablets of Destiny. Return the Tablets to me, and I shall give you control of the beasts forever. In doing so, you shall lift my curse, and I shall be free."

Loki narrowed his eyes at Kingu. "And that is all? Surely someone with your power could climb the tower and easily retrieve the Tablets for yourself."

"Not so easily," said Kingu slowly. "The curse is as twisted as this shape you see me in. It includes two riddles. The first is that the monsters have been turned viciously against me. They will do everything to prevent your climb to the top."

Loki's lips twitched. "I have my powers, too."

Kingu nodded. "You must subdue each beast to pass from one level to the next."

"How clever," said Loki coldly, touching the rune stone on his armored breastplate. "I must battle the monsters to earn the right to lead them. And the second riddle?"

Zap! The statue reverberated like a gong as Kingu's stinger destroyed the fourth mechanical bird. He turned to Loki. "The second riddle can only be solved at the summit. It is not to be puzzled out here."

Loki's eyes flared, then darkened as he touched the

stone on his breastplate again. He glanced at Fenrir, whose eyes flared as his had. When he turned back to Kingu, Loki wore a broad smile.

"My dear Kingu, I came to your Underworld for the fire monsters. Now I see my real duty is to free you from your curse! I will subdue the beasts, climb the tower, retrieve the Tablets of Destiny — and free you."

"Then come this way," Kingu said, turning his great scorpion head toward the tower. The two gods and Fenrir left the courtyard together. When we were sure they were gone, we tumbled out of the statue.

"Loki has no intention of helping Kingu!" said Sydney. "I know that creepy look. Those dark eyes. And touching his rune like that? He's probably already hatching some evil plan to use his runes to control the monsters, steal the Tablets, and betray Kingu."

Panu frowned. "You had better hope he doesn't, for everyone's sake. What did he call what he'd do to your world?"

"The Fires of Midgard," said Dana.

I looked up at the tower. It seemed a mile high, and every inch of it guarded by monsters.

"I know we're tired and scared," I said, "but we've got to get to the top of that tower."

"But you heard Kingu," said Sydney. "The beasts will do everything to stop us. Plus Loki has his runes, and all we have is a glove and a lyre."

"We can't let Loki get those Tablets," I said.

Panu frowned. "Is there really no other way to stop him?"

Fenrir howled twice in the distance.

"There isn't," said Dana, staring up at the colossal, dark tower. "Though I think we all wish there was."

Panu breathed a long sigh. "Then, come on. I'll take you to the tower. With a couple of clever shortcuts, we may even get there first!"

Jon sighed. "Lucky us."

CHAPTER FOUR

INTO THE GREAT TOWER

WE HURRIED BEHIND PANU THROUGH ONE DIM, twisting passage after another.

The air was hotter and heavier the closer we got to the tower, and all I could think of was Kingu, trapped in an Underworld where it was always night, always felt like a thousand degrees, and he was always in the body of a scorpion. What had he said?

Cursed to an eternity of darkness.

If that didn't make you want revenge, nothing

would. Still, if Kingu had warred against a greater god, wasn't he just as bad as Loki?

"Down this alley, and we'll reach the tower before Loki does," Panu whispered.

I still wasn't sure I trusted the lion-headed boy, either. Panu liked Kingu, who seemed dark and cruel, and very powerful. But all my brain could tell me was one thing: Stop Loki from finding the Tablets.

Kawwww!

A dark, winged shape dived straight down from somewhere in the upper levels of the tower, and we ducked into the shadows. Its wingspan was a good twenty feet from tip to tip. At the last second, it swooped up over the city streets, and we noticed human legs and arms among the feathers.

"Whoa," Jon gasped. "Is there a guy riding that big bird?"

"No, that's Birdman," said Panu. "Half man, half raptor, and one of the seven beasts. Beware his razor-sharp talons. This way —"

Two more passageways, an empty square, a set of steps, and finally we were at the base of the enormous tower. It seemed even hotter here. While Sydney and Jon followed Panu ahead, Dana paused next to me. Her eyes were pained, and she rubbed the wrist of her armored hand.

"Is it the glove?" I asked. "Does it hurt?"

She stared at the tower for a long second, then shook her head. "No. I mean, yeah, but it's not that. It's the Fires of Midgard. My parents read me the original myth. It's horrifying. Our world is supposedly turned to ashes. I wish I knew how the Crystal Rune is involved. I just can't remember that part of the story."

No one knew that part of the story. Maybe it wasn't even written yet. That was the problem. Or *one* of the problems.

We had so many.

"Look, if we can get to the Tablets of Destiny, maybe we can stop Loki today. And that will be the end of all this," I said, hoping I sounded convincing. "No fires. No war. No Crystal Rune. No Loki. Everything goes back to normal."

Dana looked at me, then down at the tattered book in her bag. "Maybe. I just wish I knew more."

Waiting by the archway at the base of the tower, Panu was obviously afraid. "I might be more help to you if I work my way up the outside. To there." He pointed a paw up at the tower's summit.

"Good idea," I said. "It's our mission, not yours —"

"I smell Fenrir on his way," Dana said "So we'd all better hurry."

Panu nodded. "Until I see you at the top!" With a quick wave, he galloped down a curved passage. We were alone.

"Strange guy," said Sydney. "And by 'guy,' I mean 'lion.'"

We had no time to waste, so we slipped under the arch and entered the tower. The instant I stepped into the vast open room, my limbs felt like lead and my heart sank to my knees. Dana almost fell down, her legs wobbled so suddenly. That was the effect the tower had on us.

"This tower is cursed, all right," whispered Jon, peering up at the distant ceiling. "And it's so huge."

The ground level was the distance of a dozen football fields from wall to wall, but otherwise bare. The floor was a mixture of sand and stone packed as hard as concrete, and flaming torches dotted the walls as far as we could see. The ceiling was high, and a thick rope dangled all the way down from it but stopped about twenty feet above the floor.

Jon's eyes went wide. "Are we supposed to climb up to the next level on that?"

"It looks easy enough to get under the rope," said Sydney. "But reaching it will be a different story. What are the monsters again?"

Dana flipped open her *Bulfinch's*. "Aside from Birdman and Fire Serpent, there are Thornviper and Mad Dog and . . ."

Thump-thump-thump! The floor quaked beneath our feet.

" . . . Mammoth," Dana whispered, closing the book. "Mammoth was another one."

"Mammoth?" I said. "As in the big, wooly thing that trampled cavemen —"

The floor shuddered so violently that we fell to our knees. Dana swung all the way around, aiming her gloved hand at any movement in the dark distance.

Suddenly, the room echoed with the low trumpeting of what could only have been a prehistoric beast, the ground shook again, and there was a mammoth. It was the kind of thing you'd see in a science museum. Except that he was twice the size of any fossilized museum mammoth.

And alive. Very alive.

He bounded across the floor, his shaggy black fur waving like a forest of Spanish moss. One gigantic bloodred tusk jutted out from each side of his head like medieval lances, their tips burning with blades of fire.

"Scatter!" Sydney screamed as the mammoth bore down on us.

While Dana and I took off one way and Sydney the other, Jon froze, his mouth hanging open, his eyes like saucers.

The beast seemed to like the unmoving target, because he charged full speed at Jon.

Blam! Dana sent a bolt of light at the mammoth with her glove, but it bounced off the beast's thick hide. Worse, Dana sank to one knee and clutched her quivering wrist. "Owen, the lyre!"

I pulled the lyre from its holster and plucked the strings one by one, hoping to trip the mammoth. None of the strings did anything at all, until I tried the last one. Its pitch was as low and deep as the mammoth's roar, and it reverberated against the walls.

Ooooong.

The sand on the floor rippled once, and the mammoth's tree-trunk legs slid apart. He crashed to his knees, and everything shook violently.

All of a sudden, there was a familiar stink, and Fenrir leaped into the giant room.

"Like we needed *him*!" said Dana.

Catching sight of us, Fenrir snorted, and his nostrils brewed up a fiery belch.

Loki strode in behind him, his neck gleaming with several rune necklaces. Then he saw us, and his eyes flashed in rage. "You!" he shouted. "Always you! You followed me to Babylonia? No doubt the lyre helped you somehow, but now I will end you once and for all —"

But Dana let loose a blast before that could happen. *Blam!* The force of it knocked her back on her heels, and she groaned.

Loki grabbed the flame out of the air. "Don't play if you don't know the rules, Miss Runson! I'll have that glove — and you — before this day is over!" He fired off his own bolt. I pulled Dana out of the way, and the floor we'd just been standing on exploded.

The mammoth reared up on his hind legs and let loose a roar that shook the walls. That's when I noticed that the mammoth stood a good twenty feet tall on his hind legs — the same distance from the floor to the rope.

Despite my fear, my brain was still able to add two and two. "We'll use him to get to the next level," I mumbled.

Jon looked at me, then the mammoth, then the rope, then back at the mammoth.

"That's crazy," he said.

Then Fenrir charged, Loki aimed, and Mammoth attacked all at once.

We ran.

While my fingers busily plucked the one workable string of the lyre, I glanced at Dana.

Blam-blam-blam! Bolt after bolt of silver light sprayed

across the room, and Loki and Fenrir dived away, while the lyre's note drew Mammoth to us.

With one final twang, Mammoth's fat feet skidded out from beneath him. It was enough. We grabbed his fur and hung on for dear life.

"You will not!" Loki shouted. He shot bolts at us one after another. The beast thrashed and bucked, but we climbed onto his head. Plucking the lyre's string in one ear, then the other, I steered the mammoth to the center of the room.

"Up! Up!" Sydney cried, and we leaped from the mammoth's back onto the rope. That made it start swinging wildly, which was actually a good thing because none of Loki's blasts connected with us. We climbed hand over hand all the way up to the ceiling, through the opening, and into the tower's second level.

Looking back, I saw the rune on Loki's breastplate glow and the mammoth slow to a stop. Loki tied a rune onto his tusk, and the creature bowed to him. "He got him," I said, shaking my head.

"But we got out!" said Jon, on his feet and looking around. "And we're still alive!"

I wanted to cheer, but I didn't like the look of this new level. The floor was a weird mat of thorns from wall to wall. On the far side of the room, a thick, thorny vine snaked up from the floor to the ceiling.

There wasn't a monster in sight.

"This must be Thornviper's lair," Dana said as we hurried toward the vine. "I wonder what a thornviper actually is."

Ssss . . .

We stopped, turned, and saw a tiny viper slithering calmly through the thorns. He raised his tiny head.

Ssss . . .

Sydney laughed. "Seriously? *That's* Thornviper? This little guy is one of the seven great monsters of Babylon? An earthworm could take him —"

It was a little funny. Until it wasn't.

Ssss . . . came a sound from our right. A second tiny viper.

"Twins?" said Jon.

Then — *ssss* — we saw another one. Then another, and the nest of thorns was suddenly crawling with the little things.

"Okay," said Sydney, "I get it, there are lots of them, but they're still really small —"

Then we watched as all the tiny vipers slithered together and twisted and coiled around in a mess of heads and tails.

"What's happening?" said Dana.

"I think we're seeing what happens just before we die," said Jon, covering his eyes. "Oh, no, no . . ."

Before we knew it, the little vipers had formed one single gargantuan viper.

"So *that's* Thornviper," said Sydney.

The monster reared his humongous head up to the ceiling. His fangs were as long as sabers, and they dripped goopy liquid to the floor. A tongue as long as a hallway carpet uncoiled from his mouth and snapped like a whip.

SSSSSSS!

The sound was so high-pitched I was afraid my eardrums would burst. Then a blast of flaming thorns from the creature's mouth almost incinerated us. Luckily, a weak bolt from Dana's glove was just enough to blow the flames away.

BIRDMAN

MAMMOTH

THORNVIPER

Thornviper reared again.

"Owen!" cried Dana, crouching behind Sydney and holding her wrist. "I can't —"

Oooong! The string that had worked on the level below did nothing here. In fact, none of the strings did. Thornviper rose to strike again and hissed his high-pitched whine.

SSSSS!

I twisted the tuner on the highest string to try to match the note, and the daggers of pain that shot through my eyeballs nearly made me black out.

EEEENG!

Thornviper howled in pain. All at once, a flicker, a spark — and the thorns blew up into a fire.

"Climb the vine!" cried Sydney, pulling Dana and Jon with her. "Hurry!"

We climbed the thorn vine, not caring how much it cut our fingers. As soon as we reached the top, the ceiling spiraled open. We scrambled through the opening as Thornviper wailed in his nest of burning thorns.

The floor closed beneath our feet.

We'd made it to the third level.

CHAPTER FIVE

FIGHT TO THE . . .

AS CRAZY AND NOISY AND DANGEROUS AS THE ROOM below had been, the third level of the tower was as silent as a tomb.

Which didn't make me feel any better.

We peered around and found ourselves in the center of a large ring of ascending stone benches.

"This kind of reminds me of a gladiator arena," said Dana.

"Didn't people die in those?" asked Jon.

"Only the ones who didn't win," said Dana.

Jon shook his head. "Funny. Really."

Trying to focus my throbbing eyes, I scanned the room from side to side. The ring of bleachers around us was unbroken except in two places. A long set of steps rose from ground level to the ceiling, where a low arch led, I guessed, to the next level. Next to the bottom of the stairs was a tall opening leading somewhere dark and creepy. I didn't want to know any more about that.

"So," Sydney muttered, "I guess we get up those stairs and out of here fast."

"I really like the second part of that plan," said Jon.

Before we could move, the dark opening echoed with the sound of feet, and out came an endless column of lion-headed warriors. They growled loudly, but didn't move toward us. They simply tramped up the bleachers, sat down, and began to chant.

It was *what* they chanted that was the problem.

"Furnace! Furnace!"

"I don't like the sound of that," Jon whispered.

Moments later, a large, human shape moved slowly out of the archway, and the crowd cheered louder. "FURNACE!"

"Oh, I'm going to be sick," said Dana.

We'd found our monster.

"Furnace" was eight feet of blackened metal. His legs and arms were thick, pistonlike cylinders, and his chest was as big as a tin drum. His head was a barrel with a hatch for a mouth and hot coals flaming inside. Furnace eyed us with large glowing eyes, and we backed up.

"Is he some kind of prehistoric robot?" asked Sydney, her voice shaking.

Furnace blew one big flame from his metal jaws, and the lion-headed spectators fell silent. In the sudden quiet, we heard Loki's muffled cries and Thornviper hissing below our feet. The Norse god wasn't far behind us.

"Come to me!" Furnace spat at us from his fiery jaws, coals spraying across the floor.

"We don't want to," said Jon, stepping quickly behind me.

Furnace laughed hoarsely, spit more flames, and stomped toward us. The roar from the lion-headed crowd shook the walls.

I plucked the lyre's strings frantically while we backed away from the metal monster, but none of them did anything. When I saw Dana aiming her glove, I said, "No, I'll —"

Bam! She shot a bolt from her hand, then fell to her knees with a groan, but when her bolt struck Furnace — *blang!* — he rang like a bell. The sound echoed from wall to wall, and the lyre trembled in my hands.

"That's it!" I said. I loosened one of the lyre's strings to match the sound.

When the note rang out, Furnace halted in mid-belch and wobbled on his canister feet.

"Run up the stairs!" shouted Dana.

As we rushed straight for the stairs, a wave of sand blew up from the floor and sprayed us. Furnace turned his head, and there was Loki, the runes glowing on his chest.

"Two beasts down, five more to go!" Loki sneered.

"Fenrir and the other beasts are waiting for you, Furnace. Come, be my ally. Join my war."

"Ally?" spat the metal man. "Only the holder of the Tablets commands me. Otherwise, I am the enemy of all who try to ascend the tower."

We edged backward toward the stairs.

"You are the enemy of Kingu, not of me," said Loki, the rune on his breastplate glowing more brightly. "After today, Kingu will no longer concern you. I am your master now."

The light from Loki's rune flooded the metal man.

"I told you," said Sydney. "Loki is betraying Kingu, just like I said."

"Come on!" Dana grabbed my arm, and I pulled Sydney away.

With no time to lose, we raced up the stairs to the opening. When I glanced back, I saw Furnace's massive arms drop to his sides. He bowed his colossal head. Loki hung a rune necklace on it.

"The rune controls you until I hold the Tablets," Loki said to Furnace. "Go to Fenrir and your fellow beasts below. Go!"

Furnace bowed once more, and the opening closed behind us.

"Level four," Dana said, looking around at a room carved entirely of marble. In the center of the room stood a tall, carved arch that formed the entrance to a long tunnel. Beyond the end of the tunnel we spied a ramp that ended in an opening to the floor above.

"The quickest way to the ramp is straight through the tunnel," said Jon. "I vote for the quickest way."

"Agreed," said Sydney.

As our eyes adjusted to the pale light, we saw columns on either side, and pedestals, and shelves along the walls that held what appeared to be the tattered remains of paper scrolls. We also saw loose papers scattered on the tunnel's floor.

"It looks like this place was once a library," I said.

"It does," Dana whispered. Then she stopped short of entering the tunnel. "Do you remember my parents' library? How one book was missing?"

We all nodded. The Runsons' library was where we'd first met Fenrir. We had barely escaped, but not before noticing a gap in the shelves where one book was gone.

"I think I know which book it is," Dana went on as we once more headed toward the arch. "It had a cover dotted with clear stones. It was about the Crystal Rune."

"Then your parents probably took it with them to Iceland," Sydney said.

Dana shook her head slowly. "They burned the book. I remember that."

"Burned it?" said Jon. "Why would they burn a book? They love books."

"They burned it so no one else would ever read it," Dana said. "That's why Fenrir couldn't find it at my house, and why Loki sent the Draugs after my parents. I remember my parents reading it to me when I was young." Her eyes darkened. "Not exactly bedtime reading."

"Do you remember any of the book?" asked Syd.

"A few words and phrases," Dana said. "Not much."

"Dana, your parents are smart," I said. "If they're the only ones who know where the rune is, they'll find it and keep it from Loki. Don't worry. You'll see them soon."

I had no idea what I was saying, but I hoped it sounded all right to Dana. I guess it did. She smiled a little.

"Okay," she said. "Let's keep going."

Keeping our eyes squarely on the ramp beyond the tunnel, we made our way quietly to the large marble arch. Jutting down from the top of the arch were the remains of columns that had somehow been broken. On the floor just below stood the bottom pieces of those same columns, also broken. We slipped between the columns into the tunnel.

"Weird how the walls are curved here," said Jon as we stepped deeper into the passage. "And . . ." he said, reaching out with his fingers, ". . . a little slimy."

Whooosh! Air blew over us from the dark distance, stirring the papers on the floor. It was foul, heavy, and stale. It smelled like old food. *Really* old food. Another rush of air, and the walls around us rippled. Then came something that sounded like a . . . growl.

When the tunnel shut in front of us I think we all figured it out.

"*This* is Mad Dog!" Jon yelled. "We're *inside* Mad Dog! Get out of here!"

The instant we turned around, the opening we'd come through began to close up, too, and the broken columns at the top lowered toward the broken columns on the floor. Like teeth.

We dived through the marble jaws just before they clamped shut. When they did, the arch and the tunnel shook violently, chunks of stone crashed to the floor, and there stood an enormous dog made of marble.

Mad Dog.

"Get past him and up that ramp!" I yelled.

We raced right past his humongous head, but the marble dog was as quick as he was enormous. He twisted back and swiped at us with a massive paw. His claws caught a handful of the shelves on the wall and tore them away. Then he opened his jaws wide, and flames shot out.

We all fell flat on the ramp, and the whole room

FURNACE

MAD DOG

went crimson with fire. The walls shuddered with a sound like a hammer striking stone.

And the lyre's fourth string rang.

"Thank you!" I yelled, plucking that string over and over. Mad Dog howled as if someone had smashed his big stone paw.

"This way!" Sydney cried, and we dashed up the ramp and ran as fast as we could, leaping into the darkness of the fifth level. Mad Dog charged at us one last time, but the opening to the fifth level closed, and we were alone.

A sliver of pale light shone from ceiling to floor in the distance. "Moonlight," Jon said. "That must be the exit. We're near the top of the tower."

Except that getting there wasn't going to be easy. Between us and the shaft of light was a swamp, burning with the same green flames we had seen from Fire Serpent.

"We'll have to pick our way across the swamp to get there," said Dana, scanning the tiny islands of land that dotted the swamp and stretching her glove to me. "Hold hands so no one falls in."

I took her hand. It was odd, burning and freezing at the same time. Even touching the glove for a short time made my fingers ache. I could only imagine how Dana felt.

We hopped from island to island, and the flames licked at our feet, hissing at an eerie pitch. Was that the lyre's note? It was weird how the levels of the tower seemed to be "tuned." That had to mean something, but I couldn't spend too much time thinking about it — because just then Fire Serpent rose out of the swamp behind us, rearing his fat head and snorting fire from his snout.

Jon groaned. "Here we go again. Everybody down!"

We flattened to the ground, and a blast of green flame blew over us, igniting the swamp grass. At the same time, a bolt of silver light struck the water next to us.

"Loki's back, too!" Sydney shouted.

And there he was, his face a storm of anger. Loki charged at us across the swamp. "You cannot stop me! The monsters *will* be mine! But I will take a moment to destroy you first —"

Loki threw a ball of flame at Dana, which she deflected at the last moment with a pretty weak stream of light from her glove. Loki's blast fizzled near the serpent's knobby tail. The beast spun around to the Norse god.

"You'll be bound to me soon enough, snake. In the meantime —" Loki touched the rune on his breastplate, and silver light enveloped the beast.

"Run! Over here!" growled a distant voice. I looked up to see a familiar face, standing in the distant shaft of moonlight.

"Panu?" said Jon. "You *did* come back!"

"I said I would. Now come on!" he called. "This way to the next level!"

We jumped quickly from one island to the next, when I heard Loki laugh wickedly from behind us. "You won't win this race! Serpent, stand aside! These four children are mine!"

Blam-blam-blam! Loki sprayed lightning bolts across the swamp. I hit the soggy ground, pulling Dana with me.

Ahead of us, Jon and Sydney reached Panu, and he

lifted them through the opening to the next level with his strong arms. I pulled Dana, stumbling, with me. Her gloved hand was hanging at her side. The last blast had exhausted her completely.

I couldn't get the pitch on the lyre right. The strings were tuned to the tower, not to Loki. It wasn't working.

I couldn't stop him.

Loki laughed coldly. "Say good-bye —"

But I had to try.

I pushed Dana toward Panu, swung around, and rushed Loki, swinging the lyre like an ax. Then a blast struck the side of my head, and I went down.

CHAPTER SIX

THE HANGING GARDENS . . . OF DEATH

EXCEPT THAT THE BOLT OF SILVER LIGHT DIDN'T actually hit me. It flashed so close to my face that I thought I had died. Or gone blind. Or both.

But when I looked up, Loki was stunned, wobbling unsteadily. Dana was on her knees behind me, the armored glove on her hand smoking. "That was the last time!" she said. "I can't do this anymore —"

"Then I will," Loki said, collecting himself and striding toward us, his silver hand sparking wildly.

Not thinking, I jumped up and ran right at Loki. I swung the lyre at his glove just as it flashed.

THONK! The lyre struck him, and his blast went wild. A lyre string snapped back in my face, cutting my cheek. Dana jumped up, grabbed my shoulder, yanked me around, and pushed me toward the moonlight.

Fire Serpent was tired of waiting. He leaped across the swamp at us, shrieking wildly. That was the note. I hoped that the lyre string that had snapped wasn't the one I needed now. It wasn't. The note I struck quivered like an arrow striking its target.

EEEE! The serpent crashed into the swamp with a horrible screech, splashing flaming green water over Loki. Dana and I sloshed over to Panu, where Jon and Sydney tugged us up through the opening and outside on the sixth level of the tower.

This level was a thick jungle of vines and trees and gargantuan blossoming plants, shimmering dark green and silver in the moonlight.

I gulped in the hot night air, trying to catch my breath, feeling dizzy.

"The summit," said Sydney, pointing beyond the

highest trees to a narrow stone turret that rose high over everything like a factory smokestack.

"Do you want to rest?" asked Panu, his eyes wide with fear. We must have looked pretty bad. "You guys seem . . . well . . ."

Kaaaa! Birdman circled slowly over the trees, searching for us, his black eyes scanning the jungle for any sign of movement. We were in his territory now.

I climbed to my feet and peered down at the vast, dark desert below. I could hear sounds coming from the level beneath us — the blasts from Loki's glove, the serpent screeching at the top of his lungs, the silence as Loki's runes overwhelmed him.

I thought about how many good people were in danger because of Loki's terrifying war — our families, our home, the whole world. And they didn't even know it.

There was no time.

I turned back to face the others. "That was our rest. We have to get to the Tablets of Destiny before Loki wraps his evil hands around them. Now we climb."

No one objected. They knew we had to keep going.

We tramped through the jungle until we came to a clearing that nearly surrounded the turret. Only a few scattered trees and tangled vines would cover us from above. When I saw Birdman dive to the clearing, rip up one small tree with his beak, and chew it into nothing, it was obvious that he'd made the clearing to keep anyone from reaching the summit.

"You realize that creepy bird will spot us the instant we leave the trees, right?" Sydney said. "We're going to have to run really fast."

Jon nodded quietly. "I don't know about running, but I'll try." He turned to Dana. "Do you think you can?"

Her face was lined with pain, her arm hung limp at her side, the once-silver glove now gray and lifeless. But when she took a deep breath and said, "I'm ready," I knew that Dana was a true hero, and I was so proud to be with her.

"Okay, then?" I said.

And just like that, we broke through the trees and out into the open, rushing, stumbling, and hurling ourselves across the clearing. Even though he was high in the sky, it took less than an instant for Birdman to spot us. With a mocking shriek and insane speed, he dived. As he came closer, I could see that his beak was two feet long from base to point and red as blood, streaked with dark ribbons of black.

Angry human eyes, large and dark and shadowed, stared out beneath a brow of bone and feathers as red as the beak.

"KAAAA!" Birdman snarled. Flames licked the tip of his beak.

I so wished that Dana's glove was working, but all we had was the damaged lyre. With a big *whoosh*, Birdman swooped, his daggerlike talons flashing. We scattered across the clearing, but the wind from his wings almost blew us right off the edge of the tower. We zigzagged as if we were racing through a minefield until we reached the turret.

"Up! Up!" Jon said. "It'll be easy for Birdman to pick us off, so we have to climb fast!"

Great idea. But when we grabbed the vines coiling up the side of the turret, they were so sharp they sliced our fingers. You know, because being attacked by a monster wasn't deadly enough.

Circling upward to gain speed, Birdman then dived at Sydney and Jon. His razor talons swiped and grasped, and flame flickered from his beak.

I kicked out at his head. He recoiled, then lunged at me, opening his beak wide and clamping it shut just inches from my arm. I felt the hot breeze on my face.

"No, you don't!" Dana yelled. She swung her gloved fist with the force of a hammer and struck Birdman where his ugly beak met his even uglier head. *Crack!* The upper beak split and flames leaked out. Birdman twisted back in pain, seized the glove on Dana's hand, and pulled.

She screamed.

Birdman hooted in victory. I twisted the tuner on my lyre to match the pitch of the sound and slammed on the string as hard as I could. As the note rang in the air, Birdman screeched but didn't let go of Dana's hand. Sydney grabbed Dana by the waist. Jon swung his foot out and kicked Birdman where his beak was cracked.

Birdman pulled back for a second.

Loki's glove was in his beak.

Dana cried out and went limp. Jon and Sydney held her close to the tower to keep her from falling.

LOKI'S GLOVE

Birdman flapped in a rage nearby, but he wouldn't come any closer because of the sound of the lyre. He finally scratched the air harmlessly, then fluttered away, Dana's glove still in his beak.

"Dana, are you all right?" I called frantically.

She came to and stared at her hand, then at us. "I'm free . . ." she said. "I'm free. Come on!"

Just then, Loki emerged from the level below. His rune's silver glow enveloped Birdman, and the beast fluttered down to him, dropping the glove at his feet.

"Keep going!" Dana cried, taking the lead, her hand scratched red and raw. "One last climb, and we'll be on the summit."

After what seemed like hours, we made it to within a few feet of the top. I paused to catch my breath, but there was no time. Instead, I grabbed a vine and wrapped it around my hand. Finding footing, I tugged myself up.

Even in the unfamiliar night air of the desert, the air on the summit smelled strange.

Then I remembered that smell. It was the unmistakable scent of scorpion venom.

CHAPTER SEVEN

LOST AND FOUND

A RING OF TORCHES BLAZED AROUND THE EDGE OF the high parapet.

The Scorpion King stood in the midst of them, his giant head hanging low. As far as I could tell, he was staring at the exact center of the summit roof, at a stone carved with exotic characters.

Panu bowed before him. "My king!"

I stood next to Dana, Jon, and Sydney, hundreds of

feet above the ground, while the dark Babylonian Underworld stretched for miles beneath us.

Loki shouted at the top of his lungs from the level below. A flash of silver light arced over the summit.

Then Birdman appeared overhead, a rune around his neck. With a screech, he dived down to the ground below, where the five other beasts stood with Fenrir. I knew they all had runes around their necks now. They were all under Loki's power.

"Loki's close," said Jon.

"Kingu," said Dana, stepping up to face the Scorpion King. "Loki's used his runes to subdue every beast so far, but if he gets the Tablets of Destiny, he'll control them forever. Don't betray us. Help us stop him —"

Before she could finish, the tower shook, the air rippled with energy, and Loki appeared. He stared at Kingu, then at us, then at the carved stone in the floor.

"And here we are," said Loki. He had obviously waited until he had an audience to slide his reclaimed glove on his hand. It enveloped his arm and sent a ripple of energy across his armor from head to toe. "Ah. Complete at last. My armor restored."

"This isn't the way it's supposed to happen," Sydney whispered.

"It's the Underworld," said Loki, his thin lips curling into a grin. "Nothing works the way you want it to. Come with me, Dana Runson. I have not finished with you." He grabbed her bleeding hand.

Jon, Sydney, and I stepped toward him, but Loki raised his glowing fist menacingly. "Don't be foolish. You children have already lost." He circled us slowly, pulling Dana with him. "With both the Scorpion King and me against you, you have no choice but to submit to our power."

Nearby, the Scorpion King's stingers hovered like a pair of deadly puppets on strings. The points were swollen with venom. We'd already seen what damage they could do.

They were two gods of awesome power, each with his own mission of revenge.

And we were smack in the middle.

"And now to the real business," Loki said. "Kingu, where are the seventh beast and the Tablets you promised?"

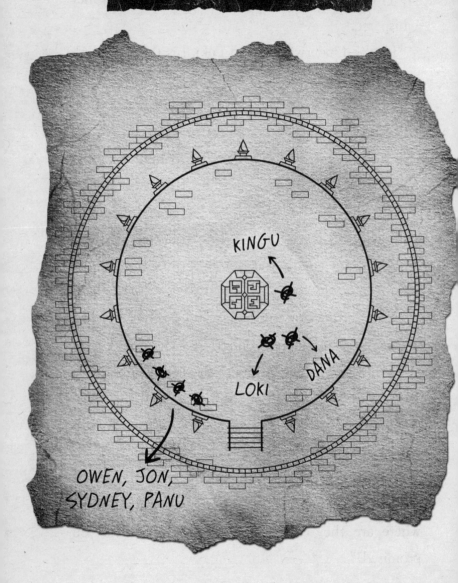

KINGU

DANA

LOKI

OWEN, JON,
SYDNEY, PANU

Without lifting his head, the Scorpion King spoke. "That is the saddest part of my curse. The seventh beast is my own son, Ullikummi, Man of Stone."

"And where is he?" asked Loki. His armor gleamed coldly in the last threads of moonlight, and the air around him was as icy as a freezer.

"Ullikummi joined me in battle," Kingu said. "He was cursed to this place with me. But the great god Marduk's spite was such that he sealed my son here, in a tomb on this summit. A tomb I have not seen until this day. My Ullikummi."

Kingu spoke his son's name as if it were an incantation. *Ullikummi.*

"A sad story, no doubt," said Loki with a sneer. "I shall regret not having your son join me. But I am here for the Tablets of Destiny. Where are they?"

Kingu's great pincers clenched and unclenched as he spoke. "The Tablets of Destiny lie under the stones in Ullikummi's arms, lost to me, lost to the world, lost . . ."

In that moment, Loki's expression turned from fake sympathy to a cold, hard, deadly look of rage. "What do you mean, *under the stones?*"

Kingu did not respond. He only repeated his last word over and over softly until it drifted into silence.

Lost . . . lost . . . lost . . .

Panu looked at me then at the lyre, and I swear my brain flashed with lightning.

Lost?

Only what is lost can be found.

Kingu didn't shift his dark eyes from the stone. "I have not seen his grave since I was cursed. By subduing the beasts to your power, Loki, you have made it possible for me to ascend the tower. I must thank you. . . ."

"*Thank* me?" Loki spat. "You can *thank* me by giving me the Tablets of Destiny! Raise them up from the ground if you have to —"

"Can you raise the dead?" said Kingu.

Standing with his back to the falling moon, Kingu was deep in shadow, his eyes invisible under the helmet of his insectlike head.

"Can you return what is lost?" he went on quietly.

The lightning flashed in my brain for a second time, and I suddenly became a genius. *Only what is lost can be found.* It all made sense! Each level of the tower had its own tone, its own musical note. That was part of the riddle and the curse. All the notes together made up a chord of notes.

The lost chord of legend.

Loki fumed, his fingers sparking like mad. "I want those Tablets of Destiny now!"

Panu stepped over to me, Jon, and Sydney. "This is the second riddle!" he whispered. "Kingu needs the lost chord!"

Looking down at the lyre in my hands, I realized something. "I only have six working strings . . . but the seventh beast has no note. He's buried. He's silent!"

Jon's eyes widened. "Owen, strum the lyre —"

So I did.

I played the six-string chord, with each string in its new tuning, and they vibrated with the notes of each level of the tower. Over and over I strummed the strings, creating a sound that swept over all of us, across the summit, down to the stones under our feet.

And under the stones, too.

"Stop that noise!" Loki snapped. "It hurts my —"

He didn't have a chance to finish before the roof

beneath our feet rumbled violently and split apart, throwing us back on our heels. Then arose a giant man of stone.

He smelled like wet sand and roots and moss and damp stone. His gargantuan arms bulged with stone muscles. His feet were three feet long from heel to toe. The stones of his joints ground together when he moved.

Loki staggered. "The seventh beast —"

In his massive, stony hands the giant cradled two flat stones carved with words that smoked as if they had just been written by a lightning bolt.

"The Tablets!" Loki said.

"Ullikummi stands before you, alive once more!" the giant thundered as he raised the smoking tablets high over his head. The skies rumbled when he spoke.

"Give me the Tablets of Destiny!" Loki said, his rune stone glowing silver in the night air. "Bow down and give them to me!"

Kingu turned to Loki. Then to us.

He bristled from legs to arms to neck to head. Fire erupted in his yellow eyes.

Then his stingers twitched.

CHAPTER EIGHT

—

TOO CLOSE TO HOME

KINGU'S TAIL HARDLY MOVED.

I didn't take my eyes off of it, but all I saw was a blur.

"Ahh!" Loki shrieked as Kingu's stinger made contact. The armor at his shoulder burst open, and we saw white bone. Loki collapsed to his knees, clutching his shoulder, and Dana stumbled away from him. I pulled her behind us.

"Kingu, you fiend —" Loki shouted, then gasped for air.

"You *dare* speak to me!" Kingu boomed, his tail arching high over his head. "You dare cast darkness upon me? I *invented* darkness, Pale Master!" He spat out those last two words as if they were a curse. Then he swung his head around to the giant.

"Ullikummi!" he said.

"By the Sun and Moon of Babylon, I obey you, Father!" the giant thundered. "What would you have me do?"

Kingu glared at Loki then, and with the slightest movement of his pincer, he indicated the ground below us, where Fenrir and the six monsters awaited. "Send the Tablets below!"

Without a pause, the stone giant threw the Tablets of Destiny from the top of the tower. They exploded like a bomb, shattering into dust at the feet of the beasts.

"NO!" Loki cried, peering over the edge of the tower in disbelief.

I suddenly understood what had just happened. The lost chord was the only thing that released the seventh monster and the Tablets of Destiny, which would free Kingu from his curse. But Kingu could never tell Loki that. So instead, he tricked him. Kingu tricked the trickster.

"My curse is ended! My son lives!" Kingu bellowed. "Loki, your childish runes cannot control me. I have tricked you. These *children* have tricked you! God for god, you do not want to fight me."

Loki staggered backward, his expression a mask of rage. Holding one silver hand over his wounded shoulder, he snarled, "You children will feel my wrath as never before. Midgard will burn to ashes!"

In a fury, he shot a bolt of silver light at us, but Kingu stepped in the way. The bolt exploded on his chest.

"You will not harm them here!" Kingu shouted. "Remember where you are, ice god. This is *my* Underworld. A world of heat!"

As he spoke, the moon fell away and the long-hidden sun edged over the horizon, a white disc of light. At the same time, Kingu's twin stingers flashed out at Loki, throwing him unceremoniously off the side of the tower.

"Ahhhh!" Loki screamed.

We ran to the edge in time to see Birdman fly up, catch Loki in midair, and carry him safely to the ground below.

Dark light shone from the rune in Loki's breast-plate, and the six monsters crowded around him.

"Monsters — to Midgard!" he yelled. Within moments, Loki had climbed in his sledge and led his snarling troop of fire monsters to the river and beyond.

We were silent at the top of the tower for a long minute.

"He got what he wanted," said Jon quietly. "He's stronger now."

"Not all of what he wanted," Kingu said. "Loki believes he has won here today. He has a few more beasts, that is all. But runes or no runes, without the Tablets, the fire beasts will not be easy to control."

The scorpion shell covering Kingu's face rippled from top to bottom, and the ridges and knobs of his forehead became less prominent.

"It begins. I become myself once more. Ullikummi, come. Children, follow!"

Stones shifted together across the summit, forming stairs that coiled down the side of the tower to the ground.

Astonished by the transformations taking place every moment to the Scorpion King, we walked behind him down the outside of the tower. Ullikummi followed, twenty steps at once.

By the time we arrived on the ground, the black dunes of night were turning pink with the coming of day.

"My curse is ended," said Kingu, one of his arms becoming a large and muscular human arm. "Soon, I shall have my revenge on the great god who condemned me. But there are more pressing matters to attend to. Loki plans to topple Asgard? Odin is a just and honorable god, well-known in the Underworlds. His overthrow will not happen on my watch." He looked at us fiercely. "This war is now my war."

"What will you do?" Sydney asked.

Kingu pointed to the west, beyond the river and the brightening dunes. "In Egypt, we will find the allies we need. Loki's journey to the northern heights shall be stopped."

"The northern heights!" Dana gasped, grabbing my arm. "I remember now! Before my parents burned the book, they locked its secret in my mind by reading me the book over and over. The legend says the rune lies in a tiny village in the far north of Iceland. I know where the Crystal Rune is!"

"Then as I go to the Egyptian Underworld, you must go north," Kingu said. "Panu, fetch the Chariot of the Whirlwind."

"Yes, sir!" said Panu, bounding away.

By the time we heard the sound of hooves thundering beneath our feet, Kingu was completely human again, his scorpion shell no more than armor. But the hooves we heard weren't horse hooves. Beasts made of rain and wind and storm approached us from the distance, their limbs whirling and howling. We stared in shock.

Panu snapped and slapped the reins wildly, then the chariot screeched to a halt. "The great chariot awaits, my friends!"

"Children," Kingu said, "in return for what you did today, the gates of the Underworld are open to you. Panu, bring our young friends to the border of the Greek Underworld. Loki will begin his attack on Midgard while his runes still control the monsters. Go in strength, children. And hurry!"

Kingu took his place at the front of his vast army of lion-headed warriors. With his giant son at his right side, they began their long march to the Egyptian Underworld.

We clambered into the Chariot of the Whirlwind, and Panu drove it like a race car driver. The chariot was as good as its name. Within minutes, we had left the vast desert behind and were standing at the banks of the River Styx.

We thanked Panu for helping us, for saving our lives, for everything.

"You're amazing," I said. "We wouldn't have gotten anywhere if it wasn't for you."

Panu grinned. "We won today, a little," he said. "Good luck, friends. I hope we meet again in different times."

JOURNEY HOME FROM THE BABYLONIAN UNDERWORLD

TOWER

CITY WALL

BABYLONIAN UNDERWORLD

BABYLONIAN DESERT

GREEK UNDERWORLD

TIGRIS RIVER

RIVER STYX

BOILER ROOM DOOR

I wondered about that. Different times could be either better or worse.

As Panu and the chariot vanished into the darkness, we hurried down the riverbank to search for the raft of the ancient Greek ferryman, Charon. Instead, we found the old man crawling on his hands and knees, barely breathing.

"Loki!" Charon cried as we helped him to his feet. "The silver brute! He's been here! Horrible monsters! A huge dog and a very ugly man with fire in his head. Loki led them up and out there. To your town!"

The old man pointed across the river, his finger wiggling at the murky darkness.

"You must go!" he cried. "Quickly!"

CHAPTER NINE

The Fires of Midgard

WE WERE BREATHLESS AS CHARON PILOTED THE RAFT silently across the river. I tipped him with one of my sister Mags's blue-haired pennies, and we rushed away through the reeds.

We were quiet as we entered the boiler room at school, quiet as we wove through the dark halls, quiet as we exited the main doors of the school.

Then we saw the fires.

"Oh, my gosh," said Sydney. "Oh, no."

Loki hadn't wasted any time.

Sirens shrieked from every direction. The horrifying winged shape of Birdman dived across the red sky, blasting flame from his cracked beak. Mammoth roared and thundered through the town, upending cars and goring them with his flaming tusks. Plumes of smoke rose from neighborhoods all around us. There were frightened shouts and screaming, car horns, house alarms, the crazed barking of dogs.

"The Fires of Midgard," I said.

Pinewood Bluffs was burning.

Past the high school we saw Furnace, howling at the top of his lungs and belching fire at the nearby movie theater. Fire Serpent stomped up behind him, his webbed feet gouging prints into the pavement. Together, the two monsters blew out red and green flames like twin flamethrowers.

We staggered back from the heat, not knowing what to do. Anger rose in my throat. I wanted to rush at the monsters and pound them with my fists, but I knew I'd be incinerated just like the movie theater. And the pizza place. And the homes across the street.

Mad Dog was at the shopping center, battering the cars one by one across the parking lot and setting them ablaze.

"Owen, is there any life left in that thing?" asked Dana, nodding at the lyre.

We no longer had Loki's lost glove. It was all up to me now.

"I have to retune the strings for our world," I said. "I need some quiet —"

"I smell Fenrir," said Sydney, waving away the ashes falling through the night air. "This way. Past the nail salon."

We ran as quickly as we could. The craft store had already gone up like a pile of twigs.

Before we got to the corner, police cars and ambulances barreled down the street toward us. It was too late to hide. The front car slowed and the window rolled down. "Kids, get out of here," the officer yelled as the car picked up speed again. "Go to your homes. Now!"

"Homes!" said Jon, his eyes wide. "Our parents. We need to find them and make sure they're safe —"

We heard the popping of gunshots and knew the police were firing at the monsters. The noise was tremendous, a roar of chaos. We had to get away from the center of town.

"I see flames in our neighborhood," said Sydney. "Where's Loki in all of this?"

Dana rubbed her wrist. "Now I wish I could sense him. Come on!"

We ran along the quieter alleys behind Main Avenue. Thick smoke rose into the black sky above us. I was so tired. We all were. I tried to return the lyre's tuning to what it was before, since we didn't need the lost chord anymore. We needed the lyre to work here. I restrung the broken string. It was loose, dull, and twangy, but at least it made a noise.

When I plucked the strings one by one, a cool breeze wafted over us. Good. It was working.

We approached the streets near Jon's and Sydney's homes. They looked deserted.

"Have they started to evacuate already?" Sydney said. "Our parents will be crazy with worry."

To see my friends stone-cold terrified struck me.

Our wild adventure in the Underworlds had seemed pretty unreal. But now it seemed too real, too true. These were our homes. Our people! Pinewood Bluffs was going to be a mountain of ash by morning.

Just as Loki had predicted.

As if she had read my thoughts, Dana touched my shoulder. "Owen, we need to find him . . . Loki . . . to . . ."

"To stop him?" I said.

And then we heard the words that no one in Pinewood Bluffs would ever say.

"Burn, Midgard! Burn!"

"There!" said Jon. He grabbed my arm and turned me toward the center of town. "He's there. On the steps of the museum."

And we saw him.

Loki stood on the top step of the museum, howling like a crazed basketball coach watching his team score.

Behind him were the double red doors that had led us to finding the lyre of Orpheus in the first place.

I didn't know what I wanted to do to Loki, but I found myself creeping along the fronts of smoldering buildings, edging closer to him.

Jon, Sydney, and Dana were right behind me. We all wanted the same thing. To stop him.

"We can get closer by going up the side," Dana whispered, nodding her head to the alley on the east side of the museum.

I smiled. "Yes."

We ducked down the alley and worked our way to the corner nearest the stairs.

I suddenly remembered the person we'd seen lurking in the museum. It seemed so long ago, but the dark figure we saw in the museum halls seemed to want Orpheus's lyre as much as we did. Who was it? It wasn't Loki. But then who?

Whoom! The night lit up with a blast of red flame, and Fenrir leaped from the shadows in front of us. The force of the blast threw Sydney back into Jon, while Dana and I ducked close to the wall.

Fenrir paced in front of us, growling loudly.

Then Loki was there, peering down from the museum stairs and grinning wickedly. "Do you like it?" he said, waving a hand at the street. "Now that Midgard burns, the war enters its final phase. Say good-bye to your homes. Your families. Your world."

He laughed a crazy laugh, like a madman. Except that he wasn't a man. He was the worst kind of god.

Evil. Ruthless. Cruel.

"You —" I said, but I didn't finish.

Suddenly, I was wrenching my arms from Sydney and Jon, pushing Dana aside, and jumping up the steps, swinging the lyre over my head like a weapon.

CHAPTER TEN

———

FLYING HIGH

Attacking Loki was both good and bad.

Even before I reached him, Fenrir threw me off the stairs to save his master from my lame attack. That was good, because it meant that Loki didn't blow me into subatomic particles.

The bad part came when I landed on the sidewalk and something cracked.

At first, I hoped it wasn't my shoulder. When I saw what really had cracked, I wished it *was* my shoulder.

The lyre frame was busted from end to end, and three strings were snapped.

Loki burst out laughing again. "A pity you take such poor care of your only weapon. Dana Runson, you will now come with me!"

"Think again!" Jon shouted, as he and Sydney took their places in front of Dana.

Loki smirked, striding down the steps, his gloved hands sparking. "Little children. Little and defenseless and —"

All of a sudden, the shriek of tires tore through the air behind us. "Kids, get in!"

I swung around.

It was my dad.

The car doors flew open, and we dived in. Fenrir leaped at the car, but Jon flung his door back out and Fenrir took a hard tumble onto the street. Loki shot a blast at us, but the car moved just in time, and it blew a hole in the sidewalk instead.

We tore off toward home — or tried to. Thornviper slithered across the road in front of us and blocked the car. The beast rose up and belched a gust of flame while my dad jammed the car into reverse, knocked Fenrir down again, and bounced full speed into a side street. We were around a corner before Loki could fire off a double dose of lightning.

"I can't believe this!" my father said. "I'm just glad you're all alive!"

We glanced at one another. Yeah, I guess we were alive. Barely.

Zigzagging left and right to avoid the flaming debris and emergency vehicles, my dad shook his head. "What is going on, Owen? Where *were* you? For hours! Have you seen these . . . these monsters? A giant bird guy. A man made of spare parts? A big dog made out of stone? It's insane!"

His cell phone rang, and he answered. "I have them," he said. "Yes, all of them. I'll be right there." I saw relief in Dad's face, but also terror as he hung up. "Your families are all at our house! Except, of course, for your parents, Dana. They're safe and sound in Iceland. But the rest of us. We were all so . . . we were . . ."

I looked at Dana. She drew in a breath.

My dad had a hundred questions for us. "Owen, was that strange man talking to you? Do you know him? What could you possibly know about any of this craziness?"

We could try to answer his questions, but that would only lead to more questions. He wouldn't understand Loki's war against Odin, anyway.

We didn't even understand it ourselves.

Sydney nodded at the damaged lyre.

As battered as it was, I hoped it still had a bit of magic in it. I plucked a couple of strings and held my breath. In those few seconds, Dad's face began to brighten.

"Okay," he said. "Okay. I guess things aren't so bad. We've been ordered to evacuate. So we'll all take a road trip up north —"

"No," I said, knowing that Loki would make his way to Iceland for the Crystal Rune. The farther they got from Loki, the better. "Not north. South. Drive south instead."

"But the police said —"

"Trust me," I said.

Dad smiled. It hurt me to see him do that, knowing that I was tricking him with the lyre. But it was better than the awful truth.

"All right, then," he said. "South it is!"

To avoid the flames, he had to drive — recklessly — away from town and along the back streets to get home. That's when I saw Mammoth near the water tower, overturning cars and setting them on fire with his tusks.

"Stop!" I said.

"Owen, there's an elephant —"

"It's a mammoth!" I said. "Please stop!"

Dad slammed on the brakes, and I jumped out.

"What are you doing, Owen?" Dana asked, rushing after me. She twisted me around to face her.

"The water tower," I said. "We can at least do something."

Ignoring Mammoth, I planted myself in front of the water tower. I thought of Orpheus and what he did. And my fingers sensed what to do. I touched the remaining four strings of the lyre one after another, repeating a short melody.

Plink-blong-ping-dooon!

The iron legs of the tower twisted slightly. My head throbbed. I almost fell to my knees from the pain, but Sydney, Jon, and Dana gathered around and held me up so I could keep playing.

"You're doing it," Dana whispered. "You're doing it!"

Another few notes, and the water tower's legs twisted too far to hold up the weight of the container at the top. The legs buckled and the tower crashed, flooding the nearby street, dousing several houses and shops. Some of the fires sputtered out. It was a start.

I heard fire engine sirens wailing closer. My father was staring openmouthed when we got back to the car.

"Okay, Dad," I said. "Now home."

A few minutes later, we screeched into the driveway and tumbled out of the car. Sydney's parents leaped on her. Jon's father dragged him from the car and hugged him close. My mother pulled in behind us, in the other car with Mags. They ran to me and Dana.

The sky was red. Smoke was everywhere. The air smelled of everything burning — wood, rubber, paint. The smell of destruction.

The Fires of Midgard were underway.

"Everyone," my father said, "we have to leave now. Owen says we should drive south. So, kids, get your stuff and —"

"We have to stay," I said, gesturing to Dana, Jon, and Sydney. This wasn't going to go over well, I knew.

"What?" my mother said. "No, you're coming with us. Dana, too. We're all leaving."

I said it again. "We have to stay here."

I thumbed the strings of the lyre again and everyone settled down, but my blood was thundering in my ears. I could barely hear myself think. Helicopters flew overhead, making the whole town a roaring, flaming nightmare.

"You guys drive south," I said. "Do it now. But . . ." I looked over at Jon, Sydney, and Dana. They all nodded. "We're staying. We'll be fine."

And even though it was the furthest thing from the truth, our parents believed it because the lyre's melody told them to.

Before she got in the car, Mom slid a letter out of her pocket and unfolded it. "I almost forgot. This was delivered today for you, Dana, by someone from school. One of the lunch ladies, I think."

Dana's trembling fingers took the letter.

As our parents went into the house to collect their things, we looked over Dana's shoulder. The note was written by hand in a script of strange letters.

"What language is that?" asked Syd.

"Old Icelandic," said Dana, looking stricken. "It says . . . my parents have left the village of Grindavik. Now they're in . . . they're in Niflheim. The Draugs found them. And there's a note."

Meet me in the woods behind the house.
— Miss Hilda

Niflheim was the Norse Underworld, a land of evil beings, frost giants, and ice dragons. The letter meant that Loki's Viking ghost warriors, the Draugs, had kidnapped Dana's parents and taken them there.

Sydney put her hand on Dana's shoulder. "I'm so sorry."

I heard more thunking helicopters over town. They hovered for a while, then made their way up the coast.

"Dana," I whispered. "Was the Crystal Rune in Grindavik? Do you think your parents found it? And now the Draugs have it?"

Dana shook her head. "The Crystal Rune was never in Grindavik. My parents must have tricked the Draugs into thinking that. But I remember the name of the village from the book they read to me. The Crystal Rune is in Thorshofn, a village north of where they were captured. Much farther north."

Sydney and Jon said their final good-byes to their parents, who then drove slowly down the street, joining the line of evacuating cars. Some of the fires were diminishing as more emergency crews arrived. That was good.

It was the only thing that was good.

I said good-bye to my parents and Mags. Then, while they packed the last few things into the car and locked the front door of the house, we hurried around to the back. We found Miss Hilda standing by the dark trees, looking up at the moon.

"Package for you. From a friend," she said, nodding to a wooden chest sitting on the ground under the trees. It had a runic symbol carved on the top.

Dana ran her fingers over it. "Sindr?"

Miss Hilda nodded. "The Norse ironsmith."

We lifted the chest's heavy lid. Inside were four helmets, four short broadswords, and four breastplates, all obviously old and obviously the real thing.

"Compliments of Odin," said Miss Hilda.

Jon gulped as he picked up one of the swords. "Are there bandages in here, too?"

"I guess this means war," Sydney said.

I looked at Dana. Her eyes were full of fear. She gave a short nod. "My mom and dad better not be hurt."

"Time to go," Miss Hilda said, nodding over her shoulder. A torch flared among the trees, and we saw several very large horses. Flying horses, we knew, because on two of them sat Hilda's sisters, Lillian and Marge, in gleaming blue armor. Lunch ladies by day, they were really the Valkyries of Norse myth.

ARMOR

"We have a horse for each of you," said Hilda. "Let's ride."

We helped one another put on the armor and followed Miss Hilda into the woods, where four armored horses were waiting. We mounted them.

"Owen?"

I turned around. My little sister, Mags, stood in the side yard, her eyes as wide as the moon. "Where are you going?"

The sky was red along the coast. The Fires of Midgard were spreading.

"I love you, Mags," I said. She looked at me. I didn't have the heart to fool her with the lyre. "Now go back to Mom. It'll be all right."

She stood for a second more, then turned and ran to the car. It was horrible to say good-bye. Especially because I wasn't sure when I'd see my family again.

Or *if* I would see them again.

"Hoyo-to*ho*!" the Valkyries chanted. Together, our horses left Pinewood Bluffs beneath us and flew quickly up into the night.

GLOSSARY

Asgard (Norse Mythology): home of the Norse gods and the court of Odin

Charon (Greek Mythology): a ferryman who leads the souls of the dead across the River Styx

Fenrir (Norse Mythology): a giant, fire-breathing red wolf

Hades (Greek Mythology): the ruler of the Greek Underworld

Kingu (Babylonian Mythology): a famous Babylonian warrior who rebelled against Marduk and was cursed with the body of a scorpion

Loki (Norse Mythology): a trickster god

Lyre of Orpheus (Greek Mythology): a stringed instrument that charms people, animals, and objects into doing things for Orpheus

Marduk (Babylonian Mythology): the great god of the Babylonian empire

Midgard (Norse Mythology): a name for the world of humans

Orpheus (Greek Mythology): a musician who traveled to the Underworld to bring his wife back from the dead

River Styx (Greek Mythology): a river that divides the land of the living from the land of the dead

Runes (Norse Mythology): old, powerful stones with magic symbols carved on them

Seven Monsters of Babylon (Babylonian Mythology): in this story, the seven monsters are Mammoth, Thornviper, Furnace, Mad Dog, Fire Serpent, Birdman, and Ullikummi

Valkyries (Norse Mythology): women who work for Odin and choose who lives and dies in battle

DON'T MISS A MINUTE OF THE NEXT ADVENTURE!

TURN THE PAGE FOR

A SNEAK PEEK. . . .

We quietly approached the frozen curtain, until we heard something in the passage behind us.

Scuffling.

Scratching.

Breathing.

"So," Jon whispered. "The mine isn't abandoned after all."

Sydney held up the torch. In its glow we could see a pack of dog-like creatures pad slowly into the cave. There must have been a dozen of them. They had no skin — just bones and teeth and skulls and slitty eyes. That glowed.

"Skeleton dogs," said Jon, drawing his sword.

"*Killer* skeleton dogs," Dana said softly.

We had no choice but to run.